To Russell & Rc

Keep Cooking up!

Jim Weller

Orv and *Willa*
FIND A HOME

JIM WELLER

ISBN 978-1-64569-957-6 (hardcover)
ISBN 978-1-64569-958-3 (digital)

Christian Faith Publishing, Inc.
832 Park Avenue
Meadville, PA 16335
www.christianfaithpublishing.com

Printed in the United States of America

To my four grandchildren, Noah, Collin, Evie, and Ruthie. I really do love you more than eagles!

For since the creation of the world God's invisible qualities—his eternal power and divine nature—have been clearly seen, being understood from what has been made, so that people are without excuse.

—Romans 1:20

With the sound of the clanging and banging of last night's New Year's Eve celebrations still ringing in their ears, two young adult bald eagles slowly winged their way above the Great Miami River in the radiant morning sunlight. As the female lands in a lone sycamore tree, she complains, "Boy, Orv, those humans sure were noisy last night!"

"What did you say, Willa?" Orv asked as he landed on the limb above her. "I can't hear you because my ears are still ringing from all that noise last night. 'Bout knocked me off of my perch! Wonder what all that ruckus was about?"

Willa just laughed to herself as she looked at her handsome mate. The sunbeams danced in the frosty air and accentuated the dark eye stripe on the side of his face. They were only four years old when they had first met just about a year ago, but their budding lifelong pair-bond had grown steadily stronger as the months had passed. Willa knew that the pretty stripe on Orv's head and the dark stripe on the trailing edge of his white tail feathers would fade away as he aged this year. She admitted to herself that she would miss them, for she thought they made him look rather distinguished.

"Are you hungry?" Orv asked, interrupting her thoughts.

"Not really. I just want to perch here and enjoy this beautiful morning," Willa answered. "You go ahead and eat."

"Yes, Dear!" Orv responded as he released his perch and glided toward the nearby river. He had learned that "Yes, Dear" was almost always the best response when Willa suggested something, although he wondered if this time he may have sounded a bit too enthusiastic as he said it. But he was really hungry!

He was also an excellent fisherman, which is a really good thing when almost all you eat is fish. He relied a lot on his sharp eyesight. An eagle's vision is amazing, way better than human vision. They can see a fish swimming underwater with no problem at all.

Immediately, he spotted a nice silvery fish swimming in the middle of the river! *That one looks tasty,* he thought to himself as he lowered his wings to their full six-foot spread. Keeping his eye on his prey, he glided just above the water's surface. As he approached the fish, he stretched his legs forward and flared his toes and talons. Then, as fast as lightning, he dipped his toes into the cold water and snatched up the fish, flying on without missing a wingbeat!

"Oh, yeah! Oh, yeah! Who's the best fisherman around? That's right! It's me!" he sang as he looked back to see if Willa had witnessed his amazing skills.

But to his dismay, his mate had drifted off to sleep in the warm sunlight. "Oh man," he whined as he landed back in Willa's tree. He said something else too; but with his mouth full of fish, he was really hard to understand.

* * * * *

After finishing his breakfast, he sat in the sycamore for over an hour as Willa slept. As he sat, he watched the activity on the river below him. Canada geese were everywhere along with a variety of ducks and other waterfowl.

The lakes were pretty frozen over right now, so this river was the place to be. As he watched, a pair of beautiful mute swans came drifting by. Orv admired their gracefulness and thought that they were almost as graceful as an eagle.

The swans made a big circle in the sky and prepared for a landing on the already crowded river. The Canada geese scurried to get out of the big swans' way, but one goose wasn't quite fast enough and almost got bumped on the head by the swans as they touched down!

Orv laughed out loud! His laughter woke up Willa. "What's so funny?" she asked.

"These two swans were… This silly goose… They almost hit… Oh, you just had to be there," Orv sighed as he snickered once more.

"Did you get something to eat?" Willa inquired.

"Yep, but I'm kind of getting hungry again," Orv admitted.

"No!" Willa sternly chided, "we are supposed to be looking for a homesite today, remember?"

"Yes, Dear," Orv conceded.

And with that, Willa flew upstream toward a nearby park.

She had noticed the park's stately trees as they had flown over them earlier; and now that she was rested, she wanted to take a closer look. Orv took one more glance at that silly goose, still smoothing its feathers as it stood on the ice, and then followed after Willa. They slowly circled over the park together.

"Hmm? I just don't know," Willa wondered.

"Hey! What's that big white egg down there? It's enormous!" Orv yelled in surprise.

"What? What are you talking about?" Willa asked.

"That big egg right in the middle of the park! Half of it is missing!" Orv explained.

"Now you're being a silly goose," Willa laughed. "That is what humans call a band shell. It is where they play music."

"Oh," Orv said shyly. He felt a bit embarrassed, and he was not at all happy with being called a silly goose.

After a few more minutes of circling, Willa descended and lit in yet another large sycamore tree.

Orv landed nearby and watched as Willa bit off a tiny piece of the tree. He wondered if she wanted to nest in it or eat it. Willa bit off a little more as Orv watched impatiently.

After several minutes, he could take it no longer. "What are you doing?" he asked too loudly.

"I'm checking out this tree," Willa explained. "Our nest must be in a tree that is healthy and strong. It will have to be tall so we can see our surroundings, and sturdy enough to support the weight of our nest, and flexible enough to sway in the wind without breaking. After all, we will be adding more sticks to the nest every year for possibly twenty years while we have babies."

Babies? Orv thought to himself. He knew that at five years of age, mature, pair-bonded eagles can start producing eaglets, but he wasn't quite sure that he was ready for all that responsibility. "What else do we need in a nesting site?" he asked.

"Well, several things," Willa answered as she nibbled once more at the tree.

"It must be near water so we can have food [Orv really liked that requirement], and it must be isolated away from too many humans."

"How about this place then?" Orv asked. "There is water on all sides of the big egg's island."

"That 'big egg,' as you call it, is what bothers me, Orv. A band shell means humans and music and an audience of more humans. This is a very important decision. Let's just keep looking." And with that, she was off and heading downstream.

"Yes, dear." And as Orv flew after Willa, he quietly muttered, "But I really would have enjoyed having music."

In no time, they had passed back over the swans, geese, ducks, and then a very noisy highway. Willa kept flying, noting the trees along the way. Now the icy river was flowing by tall buildings and under bridges.

It was here that they landed in an old tree by a highway. "These humans must really like noise!" Orv screamed over the din of a passing traffic.

Willa just ignored him as she looked around with a frown on her bright-yellow beak. She was getting a bit discouraged. That last place had looked so promising. As the eagle population continued to grow, the best sites were going fast. Quiet rural settings were hard to find, so she was hoping a nice wooded park in the city would make a wonderful place to build their new home. She knew that they should have started building their nest two months ago, and she worried that they would soon run out of time if they wanted to start a family this year. "Orv, do you think—" she stopped short of finishing her question because Orv was no longer in the tree. She looked around and spotted her mate flying above the river, hunting for fish. "Again?" she asked nobody in particular. Then, realizing that she was a bit hungry and thirsty herself, she flew down to the river and landed on a large rock.

There, she took a big refreshing drink from the cool stream and felt a little more optimistic as she surveyed the lovely river flowing by her. She had always been fond of the sound of rushing water, and the soothing flow down here on the river almost drowned out the clatter of the noisy city above. As she watched, Orv caught another fish. *He really is something,* she thought to herself.

Soon, the cold, damp stone began to chill her feet, so she flew to a nearby log to enjoy the river's peaceful cascades. There she daydreamed about what a good father Orv would be and how happy they would be in their new home. She was quite content as she stood on that log, listening to the water and thinking about what might be. That is probably why she was so startled as Orv landed beside her!

"Orv! You nearly scared me to death!" She gasped.

"Gee, I'm sorry. Here, I caught you a fish. I'm hoping that eating something might make you feel better." He smiled as he handed her his freshly caught fish.

Willa was pleased by his thoughtfulness. "Yes, Dear," she said with a wink.

For ten minutes they stood and watched the river together. There were a lot of rivers in the city, and they all flowed into this one. That meant that the food supply should be pretty consistent all year long. And even on this bitterly frigid day, the turbulent river water was not frozen over. Orv really liked the idea of always having a well-stocked refrigerator nearby.

Soon, Willa was off again, with Orv close behind.

An adult bald eagle has about 7,200 feathers, and Willa kept every one of hers looking mighty fine, and Orv appreciated it. Willa's wingspan was almost seven feet from tip to tip, larger than his own, but female eagles are typically larger than their mates. Really, what Orv admired the most about her was her fishing abilities, which were possibly as good his own, but he would never admit that out loud. If she caught a fish that was too big to carry in the air, she would use her beautiful large wings to swim it to shore with big butterfly strokes while clutching her catch securely in her talons.

They passed over some more noisy highways, then the river widened out and took on a more peaceful flow. As they continued on, they passed one more tall building on their left.

They noticed that it had two helicopters on the roof! They did not like helicopters at all because they were about the noisiest things they had ever seen! In fact, they were so noisy that whenever they saw one in the air, they always stayed far away. Willa was once again growing a bit weary of their search. It seemed like humans and noise were everywhere!

After that, the tall buildings stopped, and the landscape changed again. Orv was actually becoming more optimistic. One remaining bridge lay ahead of them before the river widened even more and curved to the right. Just at that curve, he could see a strange looking building and a very big wooded hillside with a lot of tall trees. He was just about to point out the trees to Willa when something caught his eye.

Over his left wing, Orv noticed what appeared to be some ponds! He loved ponds! He knew that ponds had water, and water had fish! When the rivers become angry and muddy, as they sometimes do, ponds remain happy and clear! Quiet ponds are like wet picnic baskets full of tasty goodies and are usually surrounded by leafy trees that provide the perfect shady spot for an eagle to nap after a big meal. Orv just had to investigate! He was sure Willa wouldn't mind, so he banked left to take a closer look.

The ponds were beautiful, serene, not yet frozen over, and full of fish! He thought about catching one, but he knew that Willa would be wondering where he had gone. While Orv was investigating the promising ponds, Willa had gotten a bit ahead of him. He spotted her still searching for the perfect tree. She was just above the river bank and following its big curve. Directly behind her was that very strange looking building.

He had never seen anything like it before, and that made him curious. He just had to get a better look!

He flew right up to the building and circled around it. It was sort of tall and really skinny, but it didn't seem wide enough to be of much use to anyone. And it looked like it was broken because it had a big hole running right up the middle of the entire building! There were some big things hanging in the top of the hole, as if someone had tried to plug up the opening to keep the building from falling apart. He had absolutely no idea as to what it might be. Orv was just about to make one more circle when he noticed Willa landing in a tree on the big hillside. Soon he was perched beside her.

"Where did you go?" she asked.

"I was just looking at some ponds over there," he answered. "Are you hungry?"

"Orv! We just ate!" a shocked Willa exclaimed. "Besides, we are looking for a nesting site, remember?"

Orv tried not to look embarrassed as his tummy rumbled. "What were those requirements again?" he asked.

"A tree that is tall and sturdy and that can sway in the wind so it doesn't break," she reminded him.

"Like this one?" Orv asked.

"And it simply must be near water," Willa continued, as if she wasn't hearing Orv at all.

"Like that river and those ponds?" he asked again.

"And it should be safely away from all those noisy humans."

"Boy, it sure is quiet up here on this isolated hillside," Orv whispered with a twinkle in his eye.

In a few moments, Willa's mouth dropped open! "Orv! I think we have found our new home!"

"Yes, dear," he whispered as he moved a little closer to his mate. "I will miss having music though."

Just then, beautiful music started ringing from the bells in that tall, skinny building. "Let's do this!" they both sang at the same time. And they did!

The ~~End~~ Beginning

So let's see what you've learned from Orv and Willa's adventure?

1. What do you call the lifelong relationship between mated eagles?
2. At what age do bald eagles get their white heads and white tails?
3. What makes up almost all of a bald eagle's diet?
4. Is the eagle's vision better than human vision?
5. Do bald eagles catch fish with their beaks or their feet?
6. Which is larger, a male or a female eagle?
7. Do eagles build a new nest every year or add to their old nest?
8. How long can pair-bonded eagles reproduce?
9. What is a baby eagle called?
10. A bald eagle's nests are almost always found near what?
11. How many feathers are on an adult eagle?
12. What is Willa's wingspan?
13. Can bald eagles swim?
14. Who knows a lot about American bald eagles?

Answers:

1. A pair-bond
2. About five years of age
3. Fish
4. The eagle's vision is much better!
5. Their feet (using their sharp claws called talons)
6. Females are larger than the males.
7. They usually add new sticks to their old nest every year.
8. For about twenty years (until they are around twenty-five years old)
9. An eaglet
10. Water
11. About 7,200 feathers
12. Almost seven feet
13. Yes, but more like humans than ducks.

14. You do! That's who!

Orv and Willa Today

"Orv"

"Willa"

About the Author

Author and photographer Jim Weller is a lifelong resident of Dayton, Ohio, and an avid eagle enthusiast. As a young child, he was captivated by the grace and beauty of these majestic birds and would search the skies for a glimpse of a soaring eagle. But there were none to be seen, for the last known eagle's nest in the city had been abandoned in 1938.

When nesting bald eagles first returned to Dayton in 2008, ending their seventy-year absence, he founded the Eastwood Eagle Watchers, a group dedicated to protecting the eagles and educating others about the American bald eagle and its trials and triumphs.

He currently serves as Carillon Historical Park's eagle expert. More can be found about Dayton's resident bald eagles by visiting EastwoodEagleWatchers. wordpress.com.

CPSIA information can be obtained
at www.ICGtesting.com
Printed in the USA
LVHW070542080921
697235LV00001B/8